Bank Street

ABOUT THE BANK STREET READY-TO-READ SERIES

More than seventy-five years of educational research, innovative teaching, and quality publishing have earned The Bank Street College of Education its reputation as America's most trusted name in early childhood education.

Because no two children are exactly alike in their development, the Bank Street Ready-to-Read series is written on three levels to accommodate the individual stages of reading readiness of children ages three through eight.

○ *Level 1:* GETTING READY TO READ (Pre-K–Grade 1)
Level 1 books are perfect for reading aloud with children who are getting ready to read or just starting to read words or phrases. These books feature large type, repetition, and simple sentences.

○ *Level 2:* READING TOGETHER (Grades 1–3)
These books have slightly smaller type and longer sentences. They are ideal for children beginning to read by themselves who may need help.

○ *Level 3:* I CAN READ IT MYSELF (Grades 2–3)
These stories are just right for children who can read independently. They offer more complex and challenging stories and sentences.

All three levels of The Bank Street Ready-to-Read books make it easy to select the books most appropriate for your child's development and enable him or her to grow with the series step by step. The levels purposely overlap to reinforce skills and further encourage reading.

We feel that making reading fun is the single most important thing anyone can do to help children become good readers. We hope you will become part of Bank Street's long tradition of learning through sharing.

The Bank Street College of Education

For Julian
—D.O.

To Sam
—J.M.

TWO CROWS COUNTING

A Bantam Book/September 1995

*Published by Bantam Doubleday Dell Books
for Young Readers, a division of Bantam
Doubleday Dell Publishing Group, Inc.
1540 Broadway, New York, New York 10036.*

Series graphic design by Alex Jay/Studio J

Special thanks to Hope Innelli and Kathy Huck.

Library of Congress Cataloging-in-Publication Data

Orgel, Doris.
*Two crows counting / by Doris Orgel;
illustrated by Judith Moffatt.
p. cm. — (Bank Street ready-to-read)
"A Byron Preiss book."
Summary: Two crows, one big and one small,
count things they see from one to ten
and then back down again.
ISBN 0-553-09741-5. — ISBN 0-553-37573-3 (trade paper)
[1. Counting 2. Crows—Fiction.
3. Stories in rhyme.] I. Moffatt, Judith, ill.
II. Title. III. Series.
PZ8.3.O68Tw 1995
[E]—dc20
94-32240 CIP AC*

Published simultaneously in the United States and Canada

PRINTED IN THE UNITED STATES OF AMERICA

0 9 8 7 6 5 4 3 2 1

Bank Street Ready-to-Read™

Two Crows Counting

by Doris Orgel
Illustrated by Judith Moffatt

A Byron Preiss Book

BANTAM BOOKS
NEW YORK • TORONTO • LONDON • SYDNEY • AUCKLAND

4

Big crow, small crow,
on the wing,
counting, counting
everything. . . .

1 ONE sun rising

2 TWO shadows gliding

9

10

3 THREE people rowing
4 FOUR trees blowing

5 FIVE cats lapping
6 SIX socks flapping

13

14

7 SEVEN herons wading
8 EIGHT geese parading

16

9 NINE farmers haying
10 TEN children playing.

Small crow, big crow,
home they go,
counting things
they see below. . . .

19

10 TEN children snoozing
9 NINE farmers snoring

8 EIGHT geese resting
7 SEVEN herons nesting

23

6 SIX socks hardly stirring
5 FIVE cats purring

4 FOUR trees standing
3 THREE boats landing

2 TWO shadows slowing

1 ONE sun glowing.

Big crow, small crow,
dreaming deep,
counting nothing,
fast asleep.